BONFIRE NIGHT FOR FLAMMABLE DRAGONS

AN OBSCURE ACADEMY STORY

LAURA GREENWOOD

© 2022 Laura Greenwood

All rights reserved. This book or parts thereof may not be reproduced in any form, stored in any retrieval system, or transmitted in any form by any means – electronic, mechanical, photocopy, recording or otherwise – without prior written permission of the published, except as provided by United States of America copyright law. For permission requests, write to the publisher at "Attention: Permissions Coordinator," at the email address; lauragreenwood@authorlauragreenwood.co.uk.

Visit Laura Greenwood's website at:

www.authorlauragreenwood.co.uk

Cover by Ravenborn Designs

Bonfire Night For Flammable Dragons is a work of fiction. Names, characters, places, and incidents are the products of the author's imagination or are used fictitiously. Any resemblance to actual persons, living or dead, businesses, companies, events, or locales is entirely coincidental.

If you find an error, you can report it via my website. Please note that my books are written in British English: https://www.authorlauragreenwood.co.uk/p/report-error.html

To keep up to date with new releases, sales, and other updates, you can join my mailing list via my website or The Paranormal Council Reader Group on Facebook.

 Created with Vellum

BLURB

Jazz knows better than to let herself get too close to fire, even if she is a dragon shifter. When she gets assigned to fire duty for Bonfire Night, she knows she has to do something or her secret will be revealed.

Idris can't stop thinking about the dragon he's been paired with for the bonfire. The only problem is that he seems to have done something to make her want to avoid him, and he's determined to find out what.

Can he help Jazz stay safe from the flames?

-

Bonfire Night For Flammable Dragons is a light-hearted dragon shifter academy m/f romance set at Obscure Academy. It is Jazz and Idris' complete story.

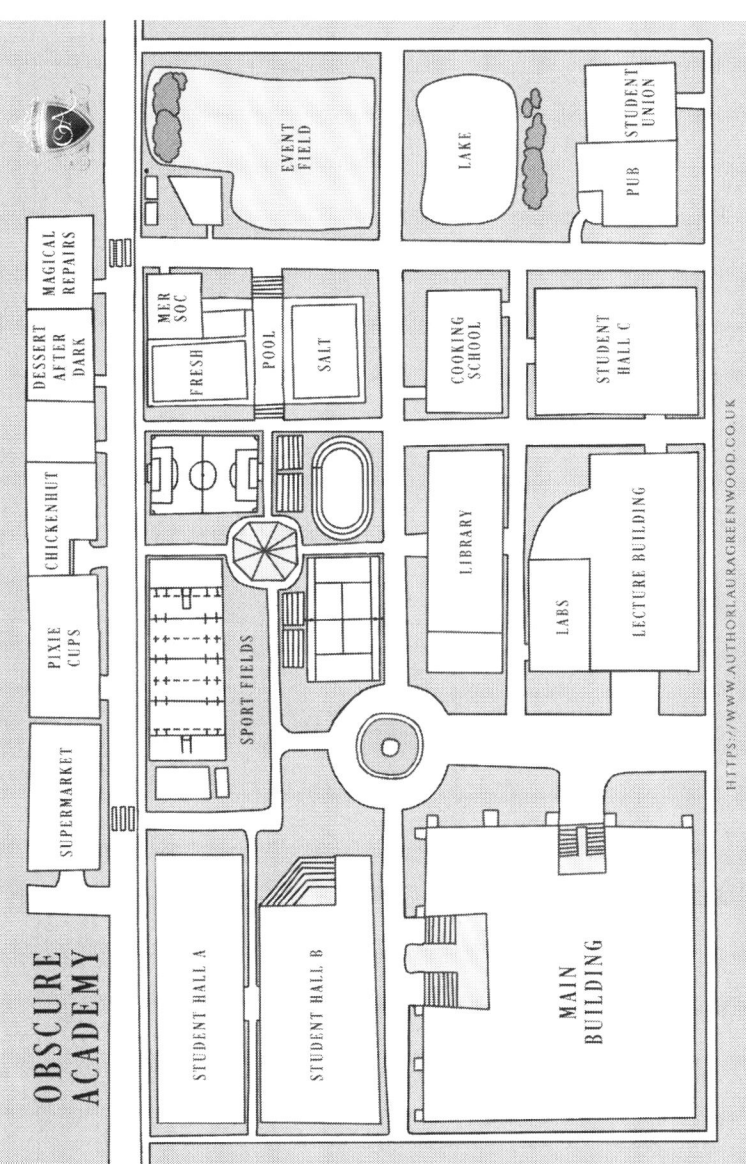

ONE

Jazz

I can't believe I'm late to DragonSoc, especially when the last thing the society chairman said last week was that we couldn't be late. Normally, it doesn't matter, but this is the day we're all given our assignments for Bonfire Night and I want to make sure I don't get a bad one.

But Zara has been drilling us hard since we lost out on the first prize in our cheer competition, which means cheer practice runs later than ever. I haven't even had time to change out of my workout gear.

I push through the door, trying to be as quiet as possible, but the problem with trying to sneak up on a room full of dragons is that it's basically impossible. I'm not sure whether we have the same genetics as non-mythical animal shifters, but we have a lot of the same abilities, including better-than-average hearing.

Several of the others glare at me as I take a seat, including Zara, who has somehow gotten here before me and doesn't have a hair out of place.

She must have flown. There's no other way.

"Ah, good, you're here, Jazz," McKenzie says from the front.

If anyone *wasn't* paying attention to me, then they are now.

"As I was saying before you arrived, you and Idris have been assigned to the fire," she continues without me saying anything.

My eyes widen.

Fire duty is *not* good news for me. I shouldn't be anywhere near it.

"Is there anything else?" I ask, sounding almost as desperate as I feel.

"No," she responds bluntly. "If you wanted a chance to say what kind of job you wanted, then you should have turned up on time."

Someone laughs further around the room, stoking the fire within me.

I sit down, realising there's no arguing with the woman in charge of organising the bonfire. She's set in her ways, and there's nothing I can do about it. I cross my arms across my chest and try not to worry about it too much. The worst that's going to happen is that I get burned. It's not like I'm going to end up in a situation that could do any permanent damage.

Or at least I don't think so. If I follow all of the safety guidance, then there's a chance it will all turn out well.

McKenzie continues giving out information about who is in charge of what, and I find myself cursing inwardly for not making more dragon friends so that I could have one of them sign me up for something better than fire duty.

Maybe I'll make an effort at the next meeting to get to know some more people.

"All right, that's everything. If you want to split off into groups, we'll get this thing organised," McKenzie says. "It's a big responsibility for us to run this, but I know you won't let me down." The implication that something bad will happen to us if we do hangs in the air, and I try not to think about it too much.

I sigh and lean back in my seat, trying to pluck up

the courage to go and talk to the person I have to tend the fire with. Somehow, I need to let him know that I shouldn't be near anything as dangerous as fire without revealing the highly embarrassing fact that I'm flammable. I have to wonder how that's even possible, but I'm too embarrassed to talk to anyone about the problem.

"You're Jazz, right?" a male voice says.

I turn to find a tall blond guy standing next to me who I vaguely recognise as being Idris. We haven't had much to do with one another until now.

"I am." I gesture to the empty seat next to me. "You must be Idris."

He nods and sits down. "I love fire duty," he admits. "It's one of the best parts of any bonfire."

"I like watching the flames." It isn't even a lie. I like *watching* fire, I just prefer to do it from a distance.

"And the crackle." A satisfied smile spreads over his face at the thought. "And we get a front row seat on Bonfire Night. It's my favourite event of the year, it has been since I was a kid."

"I prefer Christmas," I mutter.

"There isn't as much fire then." He grins.

"True, but I'm not sure why we even still celebrate Bonfire Night. I get that it was a big deal at the time, but it's been over four hundred years since

Guy Fawkes tried to blow up parliament. A lot of things have changed since then."

"True, but it hasn't happened since."

"Probably because security is better."

"Ah, so you don't think it's because thousands of effigies are burned every year on the fifth of November?"

"Does anyone really think of them as effigies as a person though?" I ask.

"I don't know whether you're just hating on Bonfire Night in general, or if you're just this kind of person." A small hint of annoyance enters his voice.

I let out a loud sigh. I should have thought about what I was saying before it left my mouth. I know better than this. "I'm sorry, it's been a long day of lectures and cheer practice."

"Ah, you're a cheerleader."

Is it me, or is there a hint of distaste in his voice?

I resist the urge to roll my eyes. It doesn't matter to some people that cheering is a sport, or that it takes a lot of different skills in order to properly pull it off. To them, it's just something people do as a status symbol, not because they love it. I won't bother correcting him. I have better things to do with my time.

Like sleep.

"If that's a problem for you, and you have

someone else in mind for fire duty, then I'm happy to swap." I don't add that it would be better for me if he agreed to that. Then I don't have to deal with his judgement, or the fire.

"No, it isn't. I'm sorry, you just don't look like a cheerleader."

I stiffen and raise an eyebrow. "What's that supposed to mean?"

"Well, you're not wearing a uniform."

"That's because I came from practice, not performing." I try not to let my frustration through my words.

"Right, that makes sense. I've never thought about it before."

"Mmmhmm." I force a smile to my face.

"Anyway, I need to go meet a friend," he says. "We should exchange numbers so we can plan the fire."

I swipe open my phone and hand it to him so he can put his number in, taking his from him in response. I type out my name and number and hand it back to me.

"Great, I look forward to working with you, Jazz."

"Likewise," I respond, though that's a lie. I'll do anything I can to get *out* of working with him. Though I suppose that's not to do with Idris himself, he does seem nice enough even with the cheerleader stuff.

Maybe we'll get a chance to work together in the future, there are only so many dragons and I have another three years at Obscure Academy to go. Maybe I'll even have McKenzie's job of assigning everything. That would be the dream, especially as it means I can avoid anything flaming.

TWO

Idris

My phone buzzes, letting me know I've got another message. I grab my phone off my desk and check the message, letting out a small groan of frustration as I read it.

< Jazz tried to get me to swap with her for Bonfire Night. >

I barely even register who the message is from. It's the fifth one I've gotten like it. She just seems to be doing everything she possibly can to get out of working with me and I have no idea why. Before the other night, we've never exchanged more than vague pleasantries.

So what can she possibly have against me?

I look out of the library window and think about what to put in a message to her, but then my gaze lands on the sports field.

Why send a message when I can go ask her in person? That seems like it will get me an answer faster, and probably a more honest one given that she won't have time to formulate a clever answer.

I pack up my books and throw my satchel over my shoulder. No one pays me any attention as I leave the library. Which I suppose makes sense. People come and go all the time, and they have no way of knowing there's an angry dragon about to explode amongst them.

At least not yet. They might if my nose starts to leak smoke, but that's only happened once, and I'm more on the annoyed side of angry than anything else right now.

All of that might change when I hear whatever excuses Jazz comes up with.

It only takes me a few minutes to get to the sports field. I've not been here before, preferring to spend my evenings studying rather than playing sports. I need the time to study if I'm ever going to make the grades I need in order to get into the post-grad program I want.

The captain of the cheer squad calls for them to

take a break, but it isn't until she turns that I realise I recognise her too. I think her name is Zara, but I've had even less to do with her than I've had to do with Jazz.

I scan the assembled squad for the dark-haired dragon I've been paired with, and am almost relieved when I spot her walking toward me.

"Hey," she says, waving once she's within earshot and acting as if she hasn't been trying to get out of our job for the bonfire.

"What have I ever done to you?" I demand.

She frowns. "What do you mean?" She checks around to make sure none of the others are listening in, but they're too far away.

"You're trying to get out of fire duty," I say. "I've been getting messages all day from dragons telling me that you're trying to swap with them."

"It's not what you think."

"The only possible explanation is that you have something against me. I want to know what it is." I cross my arms across my chest and glare at her.

"Look, it's not you. It's the job," she says. "It's not something I'm going to be very good at."

"You're a dragon," I point out.

"Yes, I'm aware of that," she responds tartly. "Do you think that being a dragon automatically makes me good at dragon-y things?"

"Shouldn't it?"

"Maybe I like swimming."

"Dragons can swim."

"Fine. Maybe I'm scared of heights and hate flying."

Despite how annoyed I am at her, I let out a small laugh. "Are you?"

"No." She softens. "But it's bad to just assume that people are good at things just because of what they are."

"True. You have a point."

"Look, we seem to have gotten off to a bad start. I have twenty minutes before we start practice again, do you want to grab a drink?"

"A drink-drink?" The surprise comes through my tone.

"Definitely not, can you imagine what a disaster it would be if I tried to get to the top of the human pyramid after drinking? That's the fast way into a coma."

"Okay, well a non-alcoholic drink is also good. Want to head to Pixie Cups?"

She nods and gestures for us to make our way towards the coffee shop often frequented by the students at Obscure Academy.

"So you're the top of the pyramid?" I ask as we fall into step beside one another.

Her lips quirk up into a smile. "I'm light to lift and I can fly if they drop me, I'm the perfect choice."

"Are you telling me you're the only flying cheerleader?"

Jazz chuckles. "No. And I'm not the only one who does the stunts either."

"Do you enjoy it?"

"Do you enjoy your hobbies?" she counters.

"I, err, don't really have any," I admit.

"You have to have hobbies. Everyone does."

"Not really. I mostly just study."

"That must be kind of boring," she says. "Maybe you have a hobby without realising it. What do you do for fun?"

"Hmm, I watch some shows."

"Anything good?"

"Dragon Survivor," I admit. "I haven't told anyone that before, it's kind of embarrassing."

"No, it's not. Loads of people love that show, otherwise, they wouldn't have had so many seasons already. What are they on right now? Seven? Eight?"

"Nine."

"Huh, I need to catch up. We've been practising more than normal, that's why I was late to the DragonSoc meeting."

"I didn't realise cheerleading was so intensive."

"How well do you know Zara?"

"The cheer captain?"

She nods. "I'm not sure who knows who in DragonSoc."

"I know of her," I admit. "But she's not someone I've spent a lot of time talking to." Or about.

"She's a great captain," Jazz says.

"But?" It's always possible to hear the but.

She lets out a loud sigh. "I love cheering, I always have, but she's at another level. She lives and breathes the team, and she wants to win the current round of competitions. Considering we only came second in the first round, she's working us extra hard as a result."

"Ah, so she's exactly like every cheer captain in every film ever?"

Jazz lets out an amused snort. "Less of a witch-with-a-b, more of an ice queen," she responds.

"Ah, that's fair." I push open the door to Pixie Cups and hold it open for her. The strong whiff of coffee seeps out of the shop, enticing us to come inside. Between the high-quality coffee and the cheap prices, it's no wonder this has become a student favourite.

"Thanks." She steps through with a smile on her face. "Do you think witches mind that we say witch-with-a-b?" she asks.

"That's a hard one," I respond. "I've never heard

any witches complaining about it, but I don't know any of them well enough for them to say anything about it."

"Good point," Jazz responds. "But maybe it's best if I stop using it just in case."

She might have a point about that.

"What do you want to drink?" she asks me.

"Oh, I hadn't thought about that. Maybe just a black coffee?"

"Coming right up," the barista responds from behind the counter. "Do you want anything in it?" She gestures to the list of magical shots on the menu.

"Just coffee, please," I respond.

"I'll have an iced tea with a shot of energy," Jazz says, pulling up the app on her phone so she can pay.

"I can get these," I say.

She shakes her head. "Call it an apology drink for making you think I didn't want to work with you," she says, reminding me of why I came to find her in the first place. "Besides, this way I get the points."

I chuckle. "Ah, so not quite as selfless as you claim."

"I'm not claiming anything." She scans her phone over the card machine and waits for it to beep.

"Okay, that's fair."

The barista sets our drinks down in front of us. "Have a good day," she says cheerfully.

"Thanks." Jazz grabs her iced tea and takes a sip. "Mmm, this is good."

"Did you expect any different?"

"No, this place is always good." I don't risk taking a drink yet, knowing that I'll burn my tongue if I do. With all of the magic available in the shop, it surprises me that nothing exists to keep the drinks at the perfect temperature. Whoever decides to do that, they're going to make a fortune. "How long have you got before practice starts again?" I ask.

Jazz checks the time on her phone and groans. "Five minutes. I swear my calves are still burning from the last move."

We start to walk back to the sports field, and it doesn't escape my notice that she's walking much slower than before, almost as if she's enjoying my company.

Which makes sense when I realise *I'm* enjoying hers. Somehow, I came to call her out on what she was doing, and now I'm chatting away as if we've known each other for much longer. I'm still not sure why she's trying to avoid working with me, but I'm starting to believe her when she said that it wasn't personal. Hopefully, she'll tell me at some point soon.

THREE

Jazz

As CONFUSING as it is to me, I come away from my coffee break with Idris with a smile on my face and feeling lighter than before. Maybe that's a strange result when he seemed to come here to tell me off for trying to get out of bonfire duty, but it is what it is.

"So, who was that?" Grace asks.

I turn to the other cheerleader, finding her standing about a foot away with her best friend by her side. "His name's Idris."

"Are you dating?"

"Grace," Krissi scolds her.

"What? He's hot, I wouldn't mind going on a date with him myself." Grace shrugs.

"We're not dating," I respond, resisting the urge to tell her not to ask Idris out on a date. I'm not sure why it even bothers me to think about it.

"You looked very cosy," Grace says.

"Ignore her, she's projecting her own relationship issues," Krissi says.

Grace lets out a soft snort. "Because not all of us find the perfect boyfriend by accidentally moving in with him."

The brunette's cheeks redden.

"But that does make it easier," I say. "And Jeremy is a catch." Even if they are the cliché of the cheerleader with the jock.

"He is," Krissi agrees.

I let out a sigh. It might be better if I can talk about this with someone. I'm not as close with anyone as the two of them are with one another, but maybe they can help me with the situation. They're normally insightful when it comes to stuff like this, even if Grace is a little boy-crazy.

"What is it?" Krissi asks, clearly catching on to my train of thought even if I didn't say anything out loud.

I let out a loud sigh. "He came here to have a go at me."

"What? Why?" At least she seems annoyed. Somehow, that makes me feel a little better about the situation.

"You know the bonfire coming up?"

Krissi nods. "We're looking forward to it, apparently it's normally a great event."

"Yeah, well DragonSoc runs it."

"I didn't know that," Grace says. "So why is the angry hot guy coming to have a go at you about that?"

"We're on fire duty together."

Krissi cocks her head to the side and studies me intently, as if trying to work out why that's a problem.

I don't blame her, it isn't immediately obvious.

"I can't do fire duty," I say. "So I've been trying to get out of it and he seems to be taking it personally."

"Why can't you be on fire duty?" Grace asks. "That sounds like a dragon's dream job."

Eurgh. I can't believe I have to say this out loud. "I'm flammable."

To my surprise, neither of them laugh.

"I can see how that would be a problem," Krissi says. "But maybe you can still do fire duty if you're just careful and don't get too near it? Or is this a case of a single spark can set you on fire?"

"It's not *that* bad," I admit. "It's just a case of I'll

burn if I touch fire like other people would. Why..." I trail off.

"Why?" Krissi prompts.

I sigh. "Why aren't you telling me that's not possible? That's always been most people's responses."

"Let's just say I understand not being good at something you should be," Krissi says.

My eyebrows knit together in a frown.

"What she's trying to say is that if she shifts, she'll fall over," Grace points out with an amused grin.

"Hey, I'm better than I used to be," Krissi protests. "But yes. I'm not particularly graceful."

"And yet you're doing something that requires a lot of balance and precision?" I can't quite wrap my head around it.

Krissi sighs. "Hold my drink," she says to Grace, shoving the water bottle in front of her.

In the blink of an eye, a leopard stands in the same place Krissi did before. She starts to walk, wobbling unevenly as she does. I have to admit that it does look like she's going to fall over.

She shifts back into her human form. "It's only a problem in one form."

"Fascinating," I whisper.

"Mmhmm. One of my flatmates is bad at potions even though she's a witch too," Krissi says. "So yeah, if you say you're flammable, I have no reason not to believe you."

"Oh." My eyes widen as the implication sinks in that while I may be weird among dragons, there are other supernaturals in the world who aren't good at what they're supposed to be doing.

"You should talk to him," Krissi says. "Tell him why you were trying to get out of it. You looked as if you were having a good conversation when you returned."

"We were, I think." Why am I second-guessing myself? I'm normally a good judge of this kind of thing, I shouldn't be overthinking it.

"Then tell him," she responds. "If you can't get out of fire duty, then he needs to know anyway so he can try and keep the two of you as safe as possible. And if he knows, then maybe he'll be able to find someone who wants to work with him on it for you to swap with. Either way, it's good for you."

"Mmhmm, I'd do that," Grace agrees."

"Tell him," I echo, sounding unsure even to myself.

"What's the worst that can happen?" Krissi asks.

"He tells all the other dragons about my problem," I mutter.

"Okay, and if he does? Will anything change?"

I frown, thinking over what she's saying. "I don't

know. Maybe they'll want to kick me out of DragonSoc or something."

"And if they do, they prove that they weren't worth your time in the first place," Grace responds in a matter-of-fact tone that's hard to argue with. "It doesn't make you less of a dragon just because you can get burned. You still transform into a big scaly thing, right?"

"More like medium size," I admit. "I'm not the biggest breed of dragon there is."

"I'm a pixie, all of you are big to me," Grace points out.

I raise an eyebrow. She's not made her species known to people before this, so it surprises me she has now. I suppose I did just tell her something about my supernatural traits. It often tends to be an exchange kind of situation.

"Size issues aside," Krissi says, cutting back into the conversation. "If anyone is funny with you about it, then it says more about them than it does about you. And it might not even be relevant if he doesn't say anything. Do you really think that he will?"

"I don't know him well enough to be sure," I admit.

"Then this is the perfect time to find out if he's worth getting to know better," she adds.

I nod, seeing her point and appreciating how much sense they're both making. "Okay, I'll tell him."

Now all I have to do is work out how. And with only a few days until the bonfire, it's a sooner-rather-than-later kind of situation.

"All right everyone, fall into position," Zara calls from across the field.

Grace lets out a sigh. "And there I was hoping that she was going to tell us we could all go home early."

Krissi lets out a soft snort. "Then you don't know Zara at all."

"Hmm, true. We should get in line before she punishes us with laps," Grace says.

I follow the two of them into place, content to put thoughts of Idris and the conversation I should have with him out of my mind, at least for the next half an hour as we run through our routine countless times in Zara's strive for perfection.

FOUR

Jazz

I SWIRL the teaspoon around the coffee in front of me, trying not to think too much about the awkward conversation I'm about to have. I know Krissi and Grace are right about telling Idris about my problem, but that doesn't make it any easier to actually do it.

But with the bonfire only two days away, I know there's no choice. I can't wait any longer.

The door to Pixie Cups opens and I look up to see Idris step inside. My heart skips a beat at the smile he flashes me when his gaze locks on mine, but

I'm not sure why. We've been messaging back and forth a bit, but I still barely know him.

Maybe it's something about the way he always smiles and gives me his undivided attention. There's definitely something nice about that.

He heads to the counter and places his order. "Do you want anything else?" he asks me.

I shake my head. "I'm good."

He nods in acknowledgement and grabs his freshly brewed coffee, and comes to take a seat opposite me.

"Hey," he says.

"Hi." I give him a weird little wave, regretting it almost instantly. Why do I have to be so awkward?

"You said you had something you needed to talk to me about?"

Disappointment fills me at him getting straight to the point, but I know there's no reason for him not to. Nor is there any reason for me to delay.

I take a deep breath. "It's about why I was trying to get out of fire duty."

He tenses.

"I know you thought it was personal about you, but it wasn't." Nerves spring to life. There are very few people I've ever told this to, but saying it out loud to Grace and Krissi helps me get past the block of not having done it very much. "It was about me. I'm flammable."

Silence falls between us, letting in the noise of the coffee shop around us. One of the machines hisses, though I'm not sure why it's doing that, I don't know enough about making good coffee.

"Flammable," he repeats, a contemplative look on his face.

"Yes. You know, when something catches fire and burns really bad."

Idris chuckles. "I know what flammable means."

"Sorry," I mutter, glancing down at my coffee. "I was trying to swap out of fire duty so I wasn't as much of a health and safety risk.

"Hmm, I see your point. Having a flammable dragon in charge of a very big fire isn't exactly a great idea."

I frown. "You believe me?"

"Is that surprising?" Idris answers, picking up his coffee and taking a sip. "For one, it's a weird thing for someone to lie about, for another, I have a distant uncle who suffers from the same thing."

"You do?"

He lets out a dry laugh, but the faraway look in his eyes suggests that it comes from memories and not my predicament. "Sorry, I didn't mean to laugh."

"What was funny?" I ask, more curious than

anything. I believe him when he says it wasn't aimed at me.

"I was just remembering Uncle Howard's antics. He sometimes sets fire to his tail to entertain the younger members of the family."

I wince. "That sounds painful."

"It does. But he says it's worth it. Most of the family is just bemused by it at this point."

"Probably with good reason. That doesn't sound healthy."

"No, but there's no reasoning with him. Everyone old enough to understand what he's doing has tried to convince him not to. Though..."

"Though?"

"I wonder if he's doing something that means the fire doesn't burn him?" He taps his chin. "I don't think that would stop him from being able to set on fire."

"What kind of thing?"

"I'm not sure. Maybe an amulet? Or fairy dust? I really have no idea, it's not something I've ever had to ask him about."

"Oh." Disappointment wells up within me. I hate the idea of not being able to do the things I'm supposed to just because of a fire risk most dragons never even have to think about.

"I could ask him, if you're okay with that," Idris offers. "I won't tell him who you are or anything."

"Not even to figure out if we're related?" The words slip out before I think twice about them.

"I suspect too few dragons are flammable for it to be genetic."

"So what do you think it is? Some kind of weird mutation?"

"I honestly don't know. Have you looked to see if there are any kinds of tests for it?"

I nod. "And there are a lot, but none of them actually tell me why I'm like this. I just had to accept that I'm a defective dragon."

"You're not," he counters quickly.

I raise a disbelieving eyebrow. "That's sweet of you to say, but not setting on fire is kind of being-a-dragon for beginners."

"Can you breathe fire?"

I shake my head.

"That almost makes it seem like the problem is with your inner fire, not with your dragon-ness."

I take a sip of my coffee in an attempt to give myself time to think. "I'm not sure what it's a problem with."

"I take it you've tried all of the normal things to ignite the flames?"

I resist the urge to roll my eyes. "Yes."

"What's the funniest one someone suggested to you? Just for fun, I'm not going to suggest that you do it again."

A small laugh escapes me. "Oh, that's hard. There was a family member who said that I should eat chillies for every single meal."

He winces. "Do you like spicy food?"

"Not anymore," I mutter. "I used to love it, but the month I tried it really put me off."

"You did it for a whole month?" he lets out a low whistle. "I'm impressed."

"I wanted to go to a big bonfire my cousins were all going to," I admit. "I didn't want to feel like I was being left out."

"Did you get to go?"

I shake my head. "My parents said it was too dangerous. And they were probably right, but it still hurt to not be able to go."

"I'm sorry."

I shrug. "Don't be. It's not like it's anything that can be changed. I don't think about it very often, if I'm honest."

"Is that why you're at Obscure Academy instead of Draco Henge?"

"Pretty much. I figured there would be fewer chances of having to tell people here, but you can see just how well that worked."

Idris chuckles, then covers his mouth. "Sorry."

"Don't be. So why did you come here? I'm assuming you have no fire-related issues?"

"I don't."

"So?"

"Promise you won't tell anyone?"

"That bad?"

"It depends who you ask. But my ex said she was going to apply here and wanted us to be together. I knew I'd have the grades to get into whatever academy I wanted to, so I didn't bother applying anywhere else."

I wince. "I can see where this is going."

"I'm sure you can. She got into Scythe Grove and basically said see-you-later."

Ah, so a reaper ex. Interesting.

"Did you try and make it work?"

"No. We had a bad argument after I found out and we broke up. I wasn't even that angry about the fact that we wouldn't get to go to the same place, it was that she didn't even tell me she'd applied."

"I'm sorry."

"Don't be. If she kept that from me, then there's a good chance she'd have kept other things from me, and that never leads to a good relationship."

"Then we can consider it a positive sign that I've

told you I'm flammable so soon," I joke before realising what I'm implying.

"We can do," he responds, not even slightly catching on.

"I never asked what you were studying the other day," I realise.

"Accounting."

I wrinkle my nose. "That sounds dreadfully dull."

He lets out a good-natured laugh. "I promise you it isn't."

"Maybe if you can make sense of all the numbers, but it just gives me a headache."

"Ah, that's a good reason not to do it. What about you?"

"Spanish."

He raises an eyebrow. "I thought you were going to say something like art."

"I'm not sure whether to take that as an insult or not."

"It isn't meant as one, you just seem very creative. Why Spanish?"

I let out a loud sigh. "Because I was good at it in school and thought it would be a good skill to have."

"What do you want to do when you graduate?"

"Now you're starting to sound like my dad."

Idris chuckles. "Sorry, you don't have to answer."

"It's fine. I was thinking about seeing if I could

change some of my modules to politics or business so I could qualify to work at an embassy."

"I hadn't considered that as a career path from languages."

"And I hadn't considered that would-be accountants might be interesting," I tease.

Idris laughs, the sound filling me with warmth. Why is it so easy to talk to him? I don't think I've ever experienced that with someone before.

Both of our mugs are empty, and he goes to get us another drink, giving me the sneaking suspicion that I'm not the only one enjoying the conversation and finding it easy.

The only question I really have is whether that makes this a date, or if I'm reading too much into it.

But I'm not quite brave enough to ask the question, leaving it for another time when I am.

FIVE

Jazz

I GLANCE at the huge pile of sticks and logs that make up the bonfire, a slightly sick feeling settling in my stomach. I'm not sure how I'm going to go through with this. I can't even light the fire, never mind do anything else with it.

Perhaps I should have gone to McKenzie and told her about my situation rather than just confiding in Idris. Not that I regret talking to him about it. I've felt a lot lighter since I have. It's not the same as telling the other girls either. As good as it was to get it off my chest with them, and even if Krissi has first-hand experience of not being great at something she should be, it isn't the same as confiding in another dragon. Not when they're the ones who can truly understand what it means to be fireless.

"Jazz!"

I turn to find Idris heading towards me, waving enthusiastically.

Despite my concerns over the fire lighting, a warm smile jumps to my face. I'm looking forward to spending the evening in his company, even if it's far from an ideal way for me to spend an evening.

"Hey," I say once he's a bit closer.

"I brought you this." He holds out a black cord with a piece of amber hanging from it.

"Thank you?"

He chuckles. "It's an amulet that should protect you from catching on fire in your dragon form. At least that's what my uncle said."

"Thank you." I take it from him and slip it around my neck. "It doesn't make me feel any different."

"I'm not sure amulets are supposed to, but I'm not sure. Maybe I should have asked more questions of the witch who made it for me."

"That's okay. I'll just be careful not to get too close to the fire just in case."

"Smart. So, are you ready?"

I look at the unlit bonfire. "Saying no doesn't exactly change anything."

"True," he agrees. "But that doesn't mean you can't say it."

"I'm ready-ish," I say. "And it'll be nice to fly."

"Me too." He takes a couple of steps back, making sure we both have enough space to do what we need to.

I take a deep breath and pull the shift out of me. My body grows and wings erupt from my back, making me about three times the size I am in human form. It's funny that Idris brought me an amber amulet when that's the colour of my scales, and even though I don't plan on getting too close, I know the firelight will glitter off them nicely.

I glance over to where Idris was standing to find a blue dragon in his place. He's slightly bigger than me, but not by much, which probably means that we're from the same species of dragon shifter, which isn't a huge surprise when I'm the most common type there is.

He gestures to the sky and I nod in response, excited at the prospect of the two of us getting to fly together. It feels special, which doesn't really make any sense. He's not the first dragon I've flown with, I've been doing it since I was barely past being a hatchling.

I leap into the air, stretching my wings with a loud snap. The cool air rushes past me and joy fills every part of my body. There's something truly magical about flying like this, and nothing I've ever done in my human form can compare.

I continue upwards, barely aware of the air growing even colder.

Idris wooshes past, reminding me that I'm not alone.

I switch directions with a quick flick of my tail, barely giving any thought to how I do it, or what makes it so that I'm able to. It's all caused by an instinct I've had my entire life.

The blue dragon comes into sight, giving me an idea. I tuck my wings in close to my body and fly in a circle around him.

He lets out a surprised cry, but then seems to realise that I'm only playing with him and changes his flight pattern so he's hovering in the air opposite me.

I'm not really sure what to do now, but solve the problem by flying quickly towards me and bumping his snout against my side.

For a moment, I'm confused, but then I recognise it for what it is.

He's inviting me to play a game of air tag.

He must see something in the way I'm holding

myself, because he chooses that moment to start flying away from me.

I don't lose another second in following him, making my body as streamlined as possible and chasing him through the air until I manage to catch him. In one smooth moment, I hit my head against his side, then use a tactic I've used to escape my cousins during this game many times.

I stop flying and let myself drop a few feet through the air, effectively taking me out of Idris' immediate reach.

It doesn't fool him for long, and we end up switching which of us is the tagger at frequent intervals. I have to admit that there was something more intimate about this than any other time I'd played the game before. Maybe it was being so focused on only one other dragon and watching the exact way he moved.

And he can move. Idris' flight is both strong and graceful, certainly awe-inspiring to watch. It's making him a formidable opponent even if neither of us can really win the game.

Eventually, he gestures his head downwards, and I know it means that it's time for us to return to the ground and light the bonfire.

I stretch my wings out as far as they can go and let myself glide gracefully down. It's a lot easier when I know the ground beneath us is mostly empty, so I can't do too much damage when I land.

Idris touches down first, making his way over to the bonfire on all fours, his tail swinging from side to side in order to aid his balance. While some dragons are just as graceful on the ground as in the sky, our species of shifter definitely isn't.

I hang back, not willing to get too close in case the amulet doesn't work.

He opens his mouth and a loud roar comes from within as a large ball of fire spews forth, hitting the kindling with a loud crash. It almost sounds as if something has gone wrong, but I know it hasn't.

The heat from the flames warms my scales. I close my eyes and enjoy it. There's something comforting about the warmth it gives off, even if I know it can hurt me badly.

We wait for a few minutes to make sure that the fire is going as well as it should be. Once Idris is confident it is, he shifts back into his human form.

I do the same, grateful for the witch-made clothing that shifts with us. I can't imagine how awkward it must have been for shifters hundreds of years ago who didn't have that advantage and just ended up naked any time they changed back from their animal form. How they managed to keep the supernatural world secret for so long is a real mystery to me. Being able to shift and fly in my dragon form without having to worry about a human spotting me is one of the things I love most about being in an open society.

"I always feel so small when I change back," Idris says as he looks up at the fire.

"I know what you mean." I close the distance between us so I can stand beside him. "Thanks for flying with me. It's been too long since I did that."

"It was fun," he agrees. "Maybe we should do it again some time?" He looks at me out of the side of his eye, as if he's trying to gauge my reaction to his suggestion.

"We should."

A smile lights up his face, but he doesn't say anything in response.

Chatter sounds from a few feet away, and we both turn to find some of the other dragons heading in our direction so they can get their parts of Bonfire Night set up.

I know this is all part of the plan, but I can't help the growing disappointment within me that my time with Idris has come to an end.

"We're still on fire duty," he reminds me, as if he's having the same kind of thoughts.

I nod and start to get myself settled for the night ahead. We still have a couple of hours before the other students start to arrive, and there's plenty to do. The fire, and the effigy of Guy Fawkes for it, are our responsibility until one of the water or ice dragons comes to put it out at the end of the night.

I'm not even sure which of them has gained that responsibility. I don't suppose it really matters when I never need anyone to extinguish my dragon flames in the first place.

SIX

IDRIS

"WILL you be all right on your own for a minute?" I ask Jazz.

She nods. "I don't think it's going to go out."

"True. And even if it does, I'll be back quick enough to do something about it," I promise.

"Would you mind getting me a water? I'm really thirsty?" She digs in her pocket and pulls out a crumpled five-pound note.

"Sure." I take it from her, though part of me wants to tell her she doesn't have to give me money, and that I can get it for her.

But this isn't a date, no matter how much our

flying games kind of made it feel like one. I've never considered whether we could have moments like that in dragon form before, but clearly we can.

I head in the direction of the stalls, glancing over my shoulder at the dragon shifter who has occupied so many of my thoughts in the past week. It's almost hard to believe that I was so angry at her when I thought she was trying to get out of fire duty. Especially when she had a very good reason for not wanting to do it. The whole situation will make me think twice next time something like that comes up.

I pull my thoughts away from Jazz, only to find them straying back moments later. Why can't I get her out of my head?

It's a silly question, but only because I know the answer to it. I'm worried about getting to spend time with her after the bonfire is over. I'm not ready to go back to being virtual strangers to one another again.

"Hey, can I have two waters?" I ask Zara from behind the refreshments stall.

"Sure." She hands them over to me.

I hold out some money.

She waves it away. "Perk of working the bonfire. You can have some sparklers if you want too." She picks up a packet.

"Sure, that'd be fun. Thanks, Zara."

She smiles and turns to the next person in line to deal with them.

Realising I've been dismissed, I turn and head back to where Jazz is waiting by the bonfire. I'm not sure if she's going to want to do the sparklers, but it sounds kind of fun.

Her whole face lights up the moment she sees me, making my pulse race and my heart feel as if it's about to burst out of my chest. Sometimes, it's hard to believe that anyone could have such an effect on me, but she definitely does seem to be.

"We didn't have to pay," I say as I hand her the water and her money back. "Apparently it's a perk no one thought to tell us about."

Jazz lets out a small laugh. "That tracks. I feel like they could have been a lot clearer on a lot of things."

"Including sign-ups?" I sit back down on the blanket beside her, glad she thought to bring it or our feet would have ached in the morning.

She let out a loud sigh. "They're probably punishing us for being first years."

"By giving us fire duty?"

"Mmhmm."

"Have you not enjoyed yourself?" I can't help but feel a little hurt by the suggestion.

"Actually, I have. It's almost enough to make me request it next year." She looks at me as if there's more meaning in her words than she's saying out loud. "Wait, have you got sparklers?" she asks, noticing them in my hand.

"Oh, yeah. Zara gave them to me. I didn't know if you'd want to do them."

"I haven't since I was a kid."

"Is that a yes?"

"That depends, are you going to do one with me?"

"That sounds fun," I say, tearing the top off the packet and pulling them out. I hand one to her.

She takes it, brushing her fingers over mine a little more than she has to in order to take it.

A lump forms in my throat.

"Oh, I don't have any matches though." Disappointment covers her face.

I clear my throat to try and rid myself of the weight of how she makes me feel. "Luckily, you have me." I click my fingers and let a small flame spring to life.

Her eyes widen. "I didn't realise that was possible."

"It isn't for everyone," I admit. "Only certain types of dragon shifters."

"No one in my family can do it. Or I don't think they can. Knowing my cousins, if they were able to, they'd have been running around and doing it all the time. They can be quite a handful."

I chuckle. "They sound it. But in this case, Dad thinks there's a different kind of dragon shifter in our lineage. Everyone on his side of the family can do it." The flame flickers and dances above my fingers.

Jazz leans her sparkler into it, letting it rest for a second until the sparks start flying out in a tiny display of light.

I let the flame disappear and hold my own sparkler to the tip of hers.

"Did you used to write your name with them when you were younger?" I ask as I swirl mine through the air to spell *Idris*.

"Of course. And swirl it around to try and get the light trails to catch themselves. I never managed to do it." She twirls her hand, a wide smile on her face as she messes with the sparkler.

I find myself grinning in response, enjoying seeing the joy in her eyes, making them glitter in the firelight.

"I used to tell my brother that his light could never catch mine," I admit. "Now I think about it, that was a bit mean of me."

She chuckles. "Perhaps. But it's all just for fun." She swirls her sparkler towards mine.

Sensing what she wants to do, I start chasing it with my own.

Jazz lets out a melodic laugh and I join in, letting myself relax into how easy it is to be around her.

Our shoulders knock together and I reach out to steady her, even though we're sitting and she's perfectly safe.

I don't pull my hand away as fast as I should, and linger in that position instead, letting the air between us grow thick with something I don't think I can name. But even if I can't, I know what it means.

Her gaze drifts down to my lips, but snaps back up again as if she's caught what she's doing.

"I'm going to go check the fire," she murmurs, sticking the almost dead sparkler in the bucket of sand pinning one of the corners of the blanket to the ground and getting to her feet.

I try to resist the urge to follow her as she heads towards the fire, knowing she isn't really going to check because it needs it.

Did I do something wrong? I feel as if something is brewing between the two of us, but maybe that's wrong.

Or she could just be surprised by the way things went and needs a moment to work out what she wants.

I let out a loud sigh. Why is this so complicated? It was only supposed to be about fire duty, and somehow I'm now finding myself worrying that I'm not going to be able to spend more time with Jazz once tomorrow comes.

The simple answer is that I need to try talking to her. It's the only way I'll know where she stands, and it'll stop the obsessing in my head.

I get to my feet, intending to go over to her and suggest we talk.

Except that everything changes when I hear her let out a loud yelp of pain. Instead of walking over, I run, hoping she's not too hurt.

"Jazz?" I call. "Are you okay?"

She turns to face me, her face set in a harsh grimace that I know to be pain. "I burned myself," she says once I'm close enough to be sure no one can overhear.

"Let me see," I say, taking her arm gently.

My eyes widen at the inflamed patch of skin on her forearm. It's worse than I expect to find on a dragon shifter, even one who says they're flammable, but it isn't the worst I've ever seen.

"Come on," I say.

"Where are we going?" she asks.

"The medical tent. Don't worry, I won't let anyone know why. This is your secret to tell as and when you're ready to."

"Thank you, Idris," she whispers. "But are we really okay to leave the fire?"

Hmm, that's a good point, and a frustrating one.

"Just give me a moment. I'll sort it out," I promise, already pulling away from her so I can go and pull in a favour with one of the others. "Just stay here and I'll be right back."

To my surprise, she nods and stays put.

At least that's one less thing to worry about.

SEVEN

Jazz

"Sit down," Idris instructs, pointing to the chair placed in the middle of the medical tent. Thankfully, there isn't anyone else here, which reassures me that we're not about to be overheard.

I do as he asks, knowing that I need the burn seeing to and this is better than waiting until I get back to my dorm room.

I roll my sleeve further back, exposing the burn more. Luckily for me, it doesn't seem to have gotten stuck to anything.

"Can I have a look?" Idris asks.

I nod and hold out my arm.

He takes it, his fingers brushing against my skin with a strong but gentle touch. Despite the sting of the burn, the only thing I could focus on was his touch.

"It doesn't look too bad," he says as he examines the burn.

"No," I agree.

"I'll grab some of the burn gel if you think that'll be enough?"

"I think so."

"Great." He lets go of my arm.

Disappointment wells up within me at the lack of contact.

He rummages around in one of the boxes and pulls out a tube and a roll of cling film before coming back over and placing the cling film on the table and uncapping the tube.

"This might sting." He pops the cap and squeezes the tube.

"Are you sure it's okay for us to have left the fire unattended?" I hold my arm steady.

"It isn't unattended," he assures me as he spreads the clear gel over the red patch on my skin.

"Who did you ask?"

"Jack. He owes me a favour."

"You didn't tell him about this, did you?" I nod to my arm.

"No. I didn't say anything about where we were going, just that we needed ten minutes. He probably thinks that we've snuck off for a quick makeout session or something."

Heat rises to my cheeks at the thought of that, though it's not unwelcome. At all.

Idris clears his throat, a slight discomfort on his face. "I'm sorry, I shouldn't have made it sound like we're together."

"It's fine," I assure him. "We could just deny it, have a public fake break-up at some point, or..." I trail off before I say what I'm thinking.

"Or?" He grabs a roll of cling film from the table next to him and gestures for my arm.

I lift it and he carefully starts wrapping it around my arm.

"Jazz?"

For a moment, I consider making something up, but I don't think that's the way to go. I just hope I've been reading the signals right. "Or we could just go on a few dates."

My heart races as I wait for him to respond, and I start to worry about what he'll say. I don't think I've misjudged the situation, but right now it feels like I may have.

"I'd like that," he says. "A lot."

"Good."

"You're all done." He lingers for a moment, not letting go of my arm.

"Thank you." My voice comes out as barely more than a whisper, causing a sense of anticipation to enter the air around us, not unlike the one we had before I got up and burned myself thanks to the stupid fire.

He reaches out and brushes my hair away from my cheek, though it's a pointless gesture considering how little my hair likes to listen to instructions.

Still, the gesture adds to the intimacy of the moment. My gaze flicks to his lips, my breathing shallow as I wait for him to lean in.

The murmur of voices growing closer from outside the medical tent breaks through the haze of my thoughts.

Idris seems to respond the same way, and pulls back.

"Sorry, I didn't realise there was anyone in here," a guy says as he pops his head around the curtain.

"It's okay, we're just about to head out," I respond.

Idris nods. "But you should take some painkillers before you do," he says to me.

"I do?"

"For the pain."

"Oh, right." Now he's mentioned it, I can feel it around the edges of the burn. Up until now, I don't seem to have been feeling it on account of the distraction.

Idris puts the supplies back and hands me a blister pack of painkillers.

"All yours," he says to the guy at the entrance of the tent.

I get to my feet and follow him outside, surprised to find how many people are now here.

"The fireworks must be about to start," Idris says.

"Ah, right. Somehow I forgot about that in all the excitement."

"The burn, or us agreeing to a date?" he asks, looking at me with a small smile on his face.

"The burn," I respond with a grin.

Idris clutches his hand to his chest. "You wound me."

"I'd have thought your skin was tougher than that," I tease.

"Only when I'm a dragon." The way he says it makes me certain he knows I'm only jesting with him. "Why don't you head back and let Jack know we'll be at the fire in a few minutes, and I'll get us some drinks for during the fireworks?"

I nod. "Sounds good."

"What do you want?"

"Surprise me."

"That's a dangerous game you're playing. What if I bring you something you hate?"

"Don't get me herbal tea, and I'm good."

He raises an eyebrow. "You dislike it?"

"I have to be in the right mood for them. And that's definitely not Bonfire Night."

"Hmm, it does call for something a bit more comforting in flavour. Leave it with me." He moves as if he's about to lean in and kiss my cheek, but pulls away before he does. "I'll be there in a minute."

"I'll see you there," I respond with a small wave.

I watch him as he walks away. I let out a loud sigh, not completely sure how we've managed to go from strangers paired together for fire duty, to on the verge of dating in so little time. I suppose it doesn't matter. People meet in all kinds of ways, and this is just ours.

I pull my attention away from his retreating form and head back towards the fire to relieve Jack from his temporary duty, barely feeling the burn on my arm.

EIGHT

Jazz

The crackle of the fire is a pleasant addition to the crisp evening air, and from this distance, it isn't likely to actually burn me again, which is something I'm grateful for. Not that I think Idris will be letting me anywhere near the fire after I managed to burn myself. I'm not even sure *how* I did that. Mostly by letting myself get distracted.

I touch my hand to my cling film wrapped arm, impressed with Idris' knowledge of first aid. Not everyone knows that's the best way to treat a burn like the one I have.

The crunch of feet against the leaves littering the

ground pulls my attention from my thoughts, and I look up to find Idris approaching with two mugs of something steaming in his hands.

A smile spreads over my face, even though it's barely been five minutes since he went in search of a drink.

"I got you some mulled cider, it sounded like the right kind of drink to go with fireworks." He holds it out to me.

"Thank you." I take it from him, our fingers brushing against one another as I do. The contact makes my whole body tingle, and from the expression on Idris' face, I'm not the only one affected by it.

He clears his throat and pulls away. "Anything need doing with the fire?"

"No. You just need to sit down so we can enjoy the firework display." I point to the ground beside me.

He does as I suggest, sitting down close enough for us to touch, but not quite doing it yet.

I take a sip of my cider, enjoying the warmth while the air is as cold as it is. I'm not sure why it's suddenly feeling so chilly, but it seems to be.

"This is good," I say. "Excellent choice."

"I hope whoever is in charge of the refreshments

isn't a final year student and can do it again next year," he jokes.

"Or they leave us the recipe."

"Would you want to do refreshments?"

"I never gave it much thought," I admit. I take another drink.

"Just that you didn't want fire duty."

"If I got to do it with you, I'd sign up for fire duty in an instant." Even as the words come out of my mouth, I know they're true.

"I'm honoured."

"And hopefully, you'll feel the same." My cider is going down easily, calling a warm glow to my stomach that spreads through my whole body. Or maybe that's enjoying the company.

I set my empty cup down next to me.

A whistle sounds from the distance, followed by a loud bang and a shower of red sparks fills the air.

The fireworks have started.

Idris puts his own cup down, and shuffles closer so he can put his arm around me.

My heart skips a beat and I lean into him, resting my head against his shoulder so we can watch.

The display continues above our heads, a symphony of bangs and shimmers of light.

"Ever wonder what it would look like from the sky?" Idris asks.

"It'll either be even more spectacular, or it'd be disappointing," I respond.

He lets out a deep chuckle, making his whole body vibrate as he does. "We can find out some time."

"But not until we've graduated and aren't responsible for this." I wave my hand to the bonfire.

"What about for New Year? Are you still going to be at the academy then?"

"I'm not sure," I admit. "I don't have any plans yet."

"Well, if you're here, maybe we could watch the New Year's firework display from the air."

"I like the sound of that." And will probably do what I can to make sure my New Year plans make it so that I can do that.

"Hey, Jazz?" Idris shifts so he can look at me.

I turn to face him, noting the intensity in his eyes.

"Idris," I say, knowing there's no need for a question.

He reaches out and trails a finger along my cheek.

My eyes flutter closed as he leans in and brushes his lips against mine.

I don't waste a moment, and wrap my arms around his neck so I can pull him closer. Our kiss deepens, the intensity stronger than anything I've ever felt with anyone before.

It's safe to say that the fireworks aren't just in the sky, and I'm welcoming them with open arms.

We break apart and I feel a wide grin spreading over my face. "I guess that's a definite yes to the date, then?"

"Was me saying yes not enough?" he jokes.

"Well, yes. But agreeing to something and actually going through with it are two different things."

"Fair point. What if I confirmed it by saying I'm free on Thursday night and I'd like to take you out for dinner?" he suggests.

"Then I'd say I'm free from six."

"It's a date," he grins.

An extra loud bang breaks through our conversation and turns our attention back to the fireworks exploding above us.

"I think we're just in time for the finale," I say, pointing to the sky.

He puts his arm around my waist and pulls me closer still.

I let out a loud sigh, content in the knowledge that this has all turned out just fine, even the burn I've gotten is minimal compared to what I feared would happen when I was assigned fire duty.

Three huge fireworks blast into the sky with shrill whistles followed by loud explosions. Red, green, and blue sparks fill the air, spreading out in a huge star. I briefly wonder what it would be like to fly between them in dragon form, though maybe it isn't the smartest thing for me to do given the fact I can burn.

I touch the amulet around my neck, only just realising I'm still wearing it. "I guess this didn't work in human form."

"I didn't think it would from what my uncle said. It's unfortunate," he says.

"It is."

"But we can try to find another way of keeping you safe from flames."

"Or maybe not. I have the cutest doctor."

He chuckles and kisses my temple, sending warm fuzzy feelings through me. I know it's too early to know for sure, but I can sense that this is going to be the start of something special.

EPILOGUE

Jazz

New Year's Eve

Idris reaches out and takes my hand in his, giving it a squeeze. "I'm glad you're here."

"You asked me to be," I point out.

"I know. But I imagine you had a lot of good offers for how to spend New Year."

"I did, but none of them are as good as this."

"Even when we haven't even dated for two months?"

"It'll be two months in less than a week," I point

out. "And I don't need more time to know that this is going to be the first of many New Year's Eves I spend with you."

He grins widely. "I'm glad you feel that way."

"Me too. What did you have planned?" I'm curious. He said it was something special, but has refused to reveal anything else.

"Remember what we talked about during the firework display on Bonfire Night?"

I nod. "Assuming you mean that it would be cool to see fireworks while in flight?"

"I do."

Excitement builds inside me. "Is that really what we're going to do?"

"It is. But first, I have a picnic dinner ready for us." He takes my hand and leads me into a small garden.

"Where are we?"

"It's a space provided by the academy for the dryads and other plant-focused fae to use. I've hired it from them for the night."

"I didn't even realise this place existed."

"Me neither until I was trying to find the perfect place for our date."

A picnic blanket sprawls across the ground, laden with all kinds of platters, and a portable stove sits off to the side.

"I thought about having an open fire, but decided it wasn't worth the risk," he admits.

"Or the fae told you no?"

"I only asked about the stove," he assures me. "But I thought it was better not to risk burning you again. That won't help me with spending more New Years with you."

"You know I don't hold that against you, right? It was just a small burn." I push my sleeve up to show him my arm without a hint of a scar. Not that I need to, he's seen it plenty of time.

"I know, but I still feel bad especially when I was so angry about you trying to get out of fire duty in the first place."

"It turned out well in the end, don't you think?" I let go of his hand and take a seat on the blanket.

"It did." He hands me a plate.

I start loading it up from the various things laid out. It doesn't escape my notice that he's chosen a lot of the dishes he knows are my favourites.

It's such a thoughtful thing to do.

We eat and chat, the conversation as easy as it ever is with him. I fill up quickly, but the amount of food on the plates surrounding me doesn't seem to go down.

"I'm going to burst," I say as I touch my stomach.

"I think you made enough food to feed us for a week."

Idris lets out an amused chuckle. "I figured we'd be hungry again after our shift."

"Good point." I'm not sure if it's all psychological, or if it's something in our bodies that actually makes us use more energy when we're dragons, but I'm often hungry after I've shifted.

It might even be something to do with the size difference between our human forms, and our shifted ones.

Idris pulls his phone out of his pocket and checks the time. "We should shift," he says. "It's almost midnight."

He gets to his feet and I get up too.

"Wait, before you do..." I reach out and catch hold of his arm, pulling him to me.

"Is everything okay?"

"Yes. But if we're going to be in dragon form, then we're not going to be able to kiss when the clock turns midnight."

"Ah, that is a downfall in my plan. We could wait and shift after. We'll miss the start of the display, but we should catch most of it."

"I like your plan," I assure him. "We'll just have to make up for it beforehand."

I go up on my toes and press my lips against his.

He responds instantly, his hand landing on my lower back and pulling me close.

It's easy to lose myself in the moment, enjoying the intimacy it brings me.

An alarm blares from Idris' phone, causing the two of us to break apart.

"Sorry, I set a reminder for us in case we got distracted."

"And that's a good thing. I could have spent all night kissing you otherwise."

"Just kissing?" he asks with a slight smirk on his face.

"You have other plans for us, so I guess you won't find out," I tease, narrowly resisting the urge to wink.

He lets out a loud laugh, knowing that I'm not serious. "Come on, we should go if we want to catch the display." He steps away from the blanket and shifts into his dragon form. He takes to the sky so there's enough room for me to do the same.

I step forward and close my eyes, pulling the shift to the forefront, changing in an instant. I stretch my wings and beat them several times, lifting myself into the air so I can follow Idris into the sky.

The sight of him hovering over the trees, waiting to lead me to the perfect spot to watch the fireworks fills me with happiness. He's put so much thought into tonight and it makes me feel so cared for.

And I look forward to starting a new year with him.

Thank you for reading *Bonfire Night For Flammable Dragons*, I hope you enjoyed it! If you want to read more about the cheerleaders of *Obscure Academy*, you can in the series of the same name, starting with *Shifting Forms For Clumsy Felines* (Krissi): https://books2read.com/shiftingformsforclumsyfelines

You can also get a bonus epilogue for Jazz and Idris for free here: https://books.authorlauragreenwood.co.uk/93kfthglfh

AUTHOR NOTE

Thank you for reading *Bonfire Night For Flammable Dragons*, I hope you enjoyed it!

I know that Bonfire Night is a strange holiday to write about when it's not really a holiday, and it's not celebrated outside the UK, but it's one of the events of the year that I love. I'm not sure what it is about it, maybe a combination of the atmosphere, the food, and the fireworks, but there is something about it. Which is why I knew that I wanted to write a story about it, and dragons seemed like the perfect choice of creature for the story.

Several of the characters who are around in this story will have books of their own, including Krissi (*Shifting Forms For Clumsy Felines*), Grace (*Minor Inconveniences For Annoyed Pixies*), and Zara (*Title to be determined*). Each of the books in the *Obscure*

Academy series is a standalone, so you can jump in and out where you like - but they're all fun-filled paranormal romances featuring students from the academy.

Or, if you're looking for more dragon shifters, you could try *Reluctant Dragon Mate* or *Charming Her Mate*, which both feature dragon shifter characters, or you could try my *Dragon Soul* series with Arizona Tape instead.

If you want to keep up to date with new releases and other news, you can join my Facebook Reader Group or mailing list.

Stay safe & happy reading!

- Laura

ALSO BY LAURA GREENWOOD

Signed Paperback & Merchandise:

You can find signed paperbacks, hardcovers, and merchandise based on my series (including stickers, magnets, face masks, and more!) via my website: https://www.authorlauragreenwood.co.uk/p/shop.html

Series List:

* denotes a completed series

The Obscure World

A paranormal & urban fantasy world where supernaturals live out in the open alongside humans. Each series can be read on its own, but there are cameos from past characters and mentions of previous events.

Cauldron Coffee Shop - Broomstick Bakery - Obscure Academy - The Shifter Season - Stonerest Academy - Harker Academy - Ashryn Barker* - Grimalkin Academy* - City Of Blood* - Grimalkin Vampires* - Supernatural Retrieval Agency* - The Black Fan* - Sabre Woods Academy* - Scythe Grove Academy*

***

The Forgotten Gods World

A fantasy romance world based on Egyptian mythology. Each series can be read on its own, but there are cameos from past characters and mentions of previous events.

Forgotten Gods - The Queen of Gods* - Forgotten Gods: Origins*

***

The Egyptian Empire

A modern fantasy world set in an alternative timeline where the Egyptian Empire never fell.

The Apprentice Of Anubis

***

The Paranormal Council World

A paranormal romance & urban fantasy world where

paranormals are hidden away from the human world, and are in search of their fated mates. Each series can be read on its own, but there are cameos from past characters and mentions of previous events.

The Paranormal Council Series* - The Fae Queens* - Paranormal Criminal Investigations* - The Necromancer Council* - Return Of The Fae*

* * *

Other Series

Purple Oasis (with Arizona Tape) - Grimm Academy - Beyond The Curse* - Untold Tales* - The Dragon Duels* - Speed Dating With The Denizens Of The Underworld (shared world) - Seven Wardens* (with Skye MacKinnon) - Tales Of Clan Robbins (co-written with L.A. Boruff) - Firehouse Witches* (with Lacey Carter Andersen & L.A. Boruff) - Valentine Pride* (with Lainie Anderson) - Magic and Metaphysics Academy* (with Lainie Anderson)

* * *

Twin Souls Universe

A paranormal romance & urban fantasy world co-written with Arizona Tape. Each series can be read on its own, but there are cameos from past characters and mentions of previous events.

Amethyst's Wand Shop Mysteries - Twin Souls* - The Vampire Detective*

ABOUT LAURA GREENWOOD

Laura is a USA Today Bestselling Author of paranormal, fantasy, urban fantasy, and contemporary romance. When she's not writing, she drinks a lot of tea, tries to resist French macarons, and works towards a diploma in Egyptology. She lives in the UK, where most of her books are set. Laura specialises in quick reads, whether you're looking for a swoonworthy romance for the bath, or an action-packed adventure for your latest journey, you'll find the perfect match amongst her books!

Follow the Author

- Website: www.authorlauragreenwood.co.uk
- Mailing List: www.authorlauragreenwood.co.uk/p/mailing-list-sign-up.html
- Facebook Group: http://facebook.com/groups/theparanormalcouncil

- Facebook Page: http://facebook.com/authorlauragreenwood
- Bookbub: www.bookbub.com/authors/laura-greenwood

Printed by Amazon Italia Logistica S.r.l.
Torrazza Piemonte (TO), Italy